colors

a book by John J. Reiss

Bradbury Press • New York

Bradbury Press
An Affiliate of Macmillan, Inc.
866 Third Avenue, New York, NY 10022
Collier Macmillan Canada, Inc.
Manufactured in the United States of America

20 19 18 17 16 15 14 13 12

Library of Congress Catalog Card Number: 69-13653
ISBN 0-02-776130-4
The typeface used in this book is Helvetica.

To Josef and Anni Albers

red

strawberries

raspberries

apples

fireman's hat

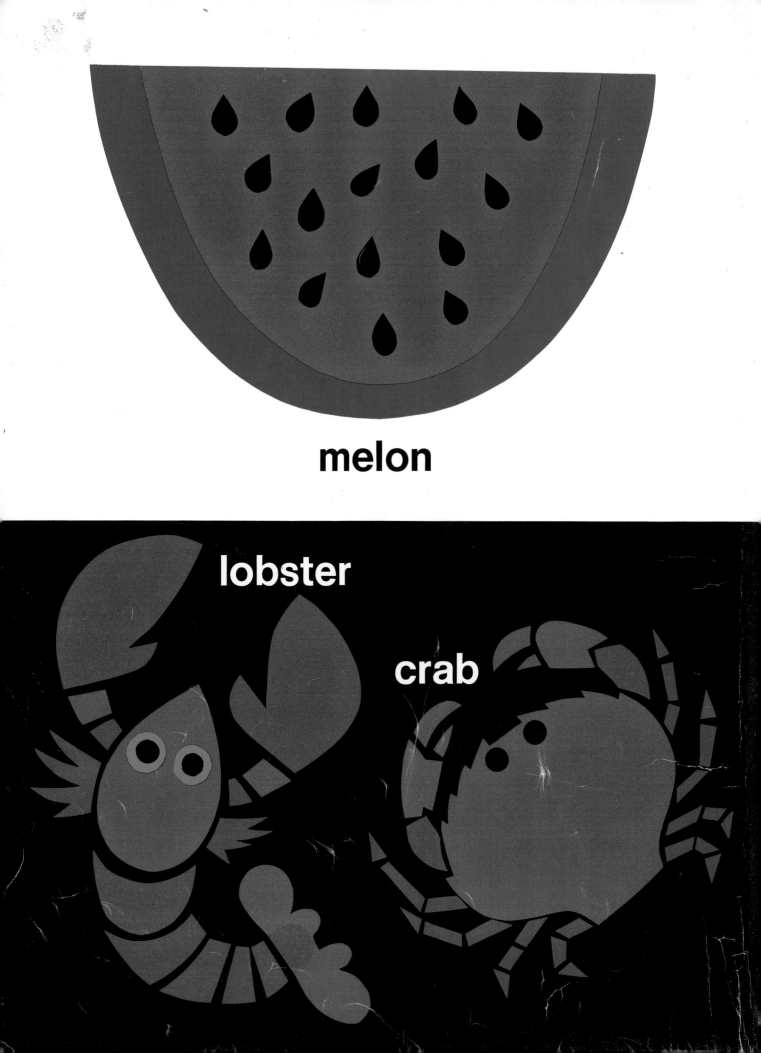

melon

lobster

crab

peppers

tomatoes

yellow

baby chicks

lemons

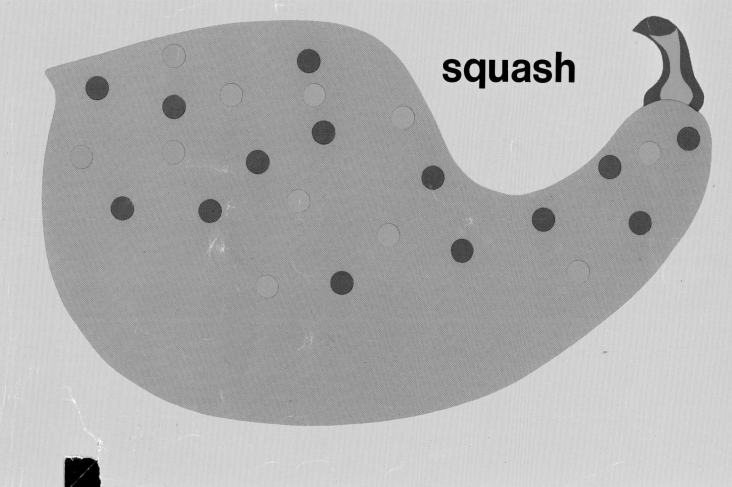

squash

bumblebees

bananas

buttercups

daffodils

daisies

cornflowers

blueberries

bluebirds

butterflies

policeman's coat

orange

pumpkin

tiger's tail

robins

goldfish

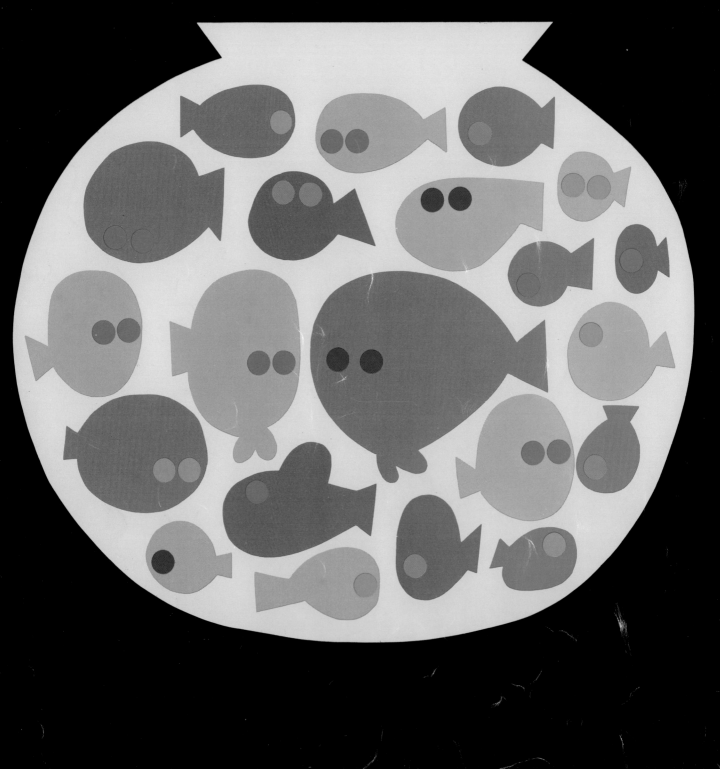

oranges

foxes

leaves

green

grass

snake

frogs

turtles

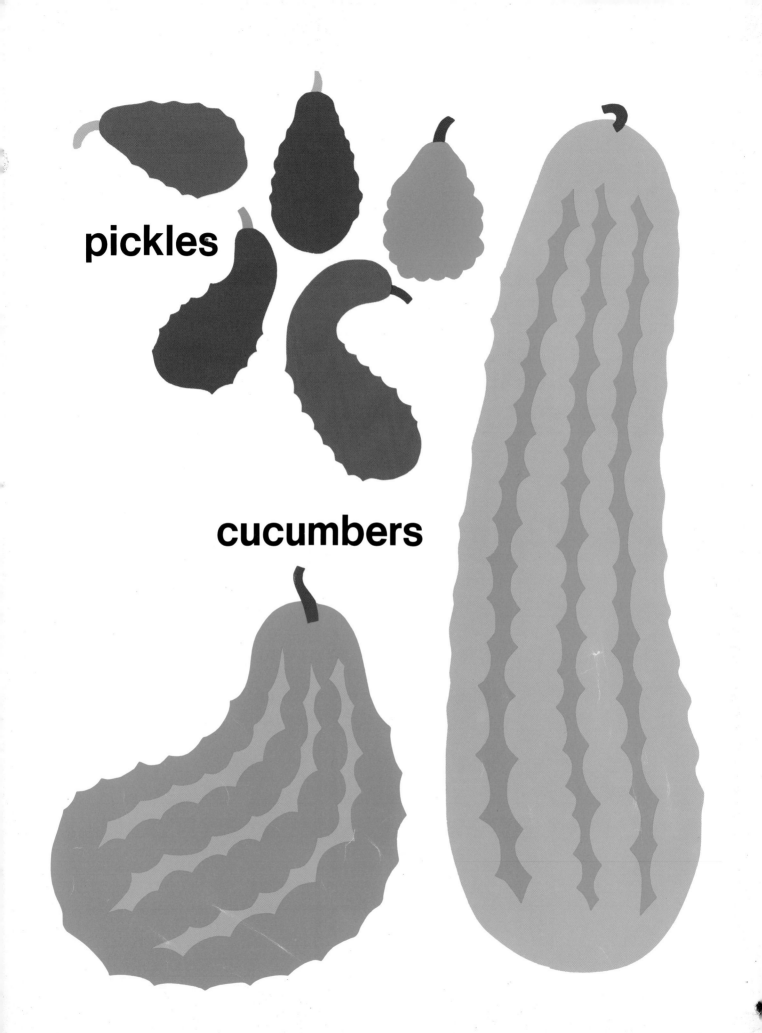

pickles

cucumbers

gooseberries

peas in a pod

purple

cabbage

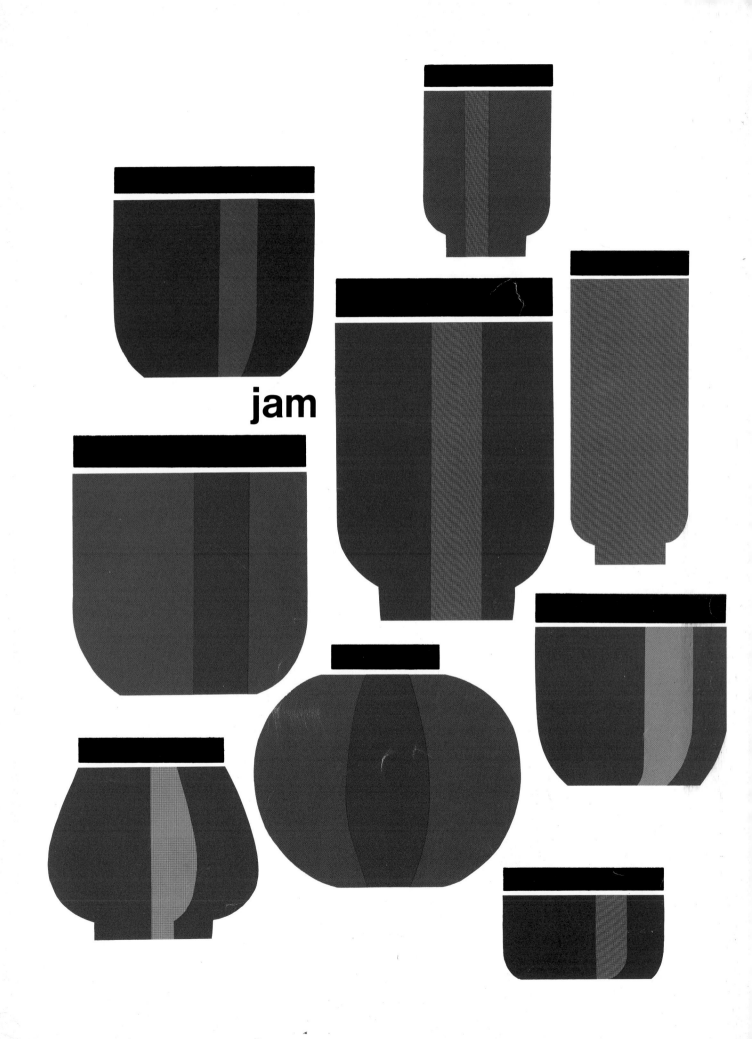

jam

eggplant

grapes

lilacs

violets

brown

fiddle

bear

walrus

snails

puppy-dog tails

licorice sticks

black

zebra

blackberries

penguins